Bug Boy

Carol Sonenklar

ILLUSTRATED BY BETSY LEWIN

A Yearling Book

Published by
Bantam Doubleday Dell Books for Young Readers
a division of
Bantam Doubleday Dell Publishing Group, Inc.
1540 Broadway
New York, New York 10036

Visit us on the Web! www.bdd.com

**Educators and librarians, visit the BDD Teacher's
Resource Center at www.bdd.com/teachers**

ISBN: 0-440-41465-2

Reprinted by arrangement with Henry Holt and Company, Inc.

Printed in the United States of America

October 1998

10 9 8 7 6 5 4 3 2 1

OPM

For Sam, the original "Bug Boy"

—C. S.

For Alex Simon-Fox

—B. L.

Contents

Going Buggy

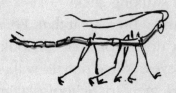

I was frozen. Arms and legs rigid. Every bit of my concentration was focused on my body.

Don't move a muscle.

It was after school and this was a spur-of-the-moment game of freeze tag, Mrs. Greene's third grade versus Mr. Carleton's. I caught my friend Suzanne's eye and willed my lips not to smile. Freeze-tag rules were ruthlessly serious—if any part of you is caught moving, you're out. I tried to control my breathing because it was fast, causing my glow-in-the-dark spider T-shirt to move backward and forward.

Suddenly, from the extreme corner of my eye, something moved at my feet. Something pretty big. I dropped my eyes as low as I possibly could. All I could see was a bunch of twigs, weeds, wads of old chewing gum, and other kinds of garbage that I didn't care to think about.

Back to the game.

There! Whatever it was moved again. My eyes were starting to cross from the strain of staring down without moving my head.

HOLY BALONEY!

A walking stick!

And a big one at that. Forgetting about the game, I bent down for a closer look. I could hardly believe my eyes. A live female walking stick on the McDowell Elementary School playground.

Next to me, I heard the usual sighs and groans. Someone piped up. "Oh great, Bug Boy is wrecking the game again."

I didn't care. For me, bugs are always, without exception, number one—everything else comes second. And I had never seen a live walking stick before—just dead ones at the Insect Museum and in books and catalogs. This was amazing.

"Hey guys! Come over here!" I yelled.

"Wow!" said Suzanne Dimarian, who was next to me almost immediately. "That is the coolest bug I've ever seen." Suzanne has been my best friend and bug buddy ever since the day I tripped over her on the sidewalk near my house as she watched an ant carry a dead grasshopper back to its colony. That was back in kindergarten. Lately, though, we haven't

4

done nearly as much bug hunting as we used to be-cause Suzanne has been hanging around with these two bossy girls in our class who think that "all-bugs-are-gross-and-disgusting." Don't ask me why. Any-one who thinks a bug as beautiful as a walking stick is gross and disgusting is beyond me.

"Awesome!" said Danny Borofsky who sat behind me in class. "It looks like a real . . . walking . . . stick!" Danny can be a little slow sometimes.

"Duh," said Raymond Wintertree, in a low voice, because even though he acted like the class Goody Two-shoes he couldn't stand it when someone found anything neat. Raymond always dressed as if he were going to a fancy girl's birthday party, and he made pictures of "I love Mrs. Greene" all the time, with a red heart for the *love*. Yesterday he tattled to Mrs. Greene when a pill bug that I'd found during recess got away from me in class and started crawling near his foot. Mrs. Greene had just warned me about bringing bugs from the playground into class. So when she saw the pill bug I was sent down to Mr. Baxter's office for a "little chat." Unfortunately, Mr. Baxter didn't agree with me that bringing in bugs from the playground was educational. But at least he didn't call my parents. Raymond's goal in life is to get other kids in trouble. I get the added bonus of being tattled on twenty-four hours a day because Raymond lives two doors down from me. Lucky, huh?

I didn't even know why Raymond was here, looking at the walking stick, since a bug as small as a velvet mite would make him run—and he certainly wasn't invited to play freeze tag. Suzanne and I called him "Pain-In" Wintertree.

By this time even the kids who'd groaned were crowding around me. Suzanne was making a path for the insect to walk. The walking stick was beautiful—dark brown, about two inches long. Its six legs were so thin and fragile looking it seemed incredible to me that it could survive at all.

"Where's its head?" asked a boy from Mr. Carleton's class.

"It's here." I pointed to one end of the stick's body with what looked like strings coming out of it. "You can tell because of the antennae. The antennae are at the head."

Everyone was quiet as we watched the insect pick its way over a Twinkie wrapper. Suzanne had gone back to her sissy friends but was watching me on her tiptoes.

"The antennae help it sense food. Right, Charlie?" asked Danny.

I nodded. "Danger, too." I hope I didn't sound like a know-it-all.

But in fact I do know a lot about bugs, as you've probably guessed by now. In fact, "Bug Boy" is a name Suzanne made up for me, and it's what I usually go by. I don't know what got me hooked, but now I just can't get enough of six-legged creatures. I love the names—assassin bug, stinkbug, shield bug, firefly, praying mantis, cicada, dragonfly, damselfly, grasshopper, luna moth, water striders—for starters. I love the way they look, their colors and shapes and sizes, and the amazingly cool things they can do. It's as if each insect has its own unique special power— like the grasshopper's hop, the stinkbug's smell, or the cricket's chirp—that makes them superheroes of the animal world.

I've read every bug book in the library, most twice. I've been to the Insect Museum so many times they finally got a stool with wheels on it so I wouldn't drag chairs around to see the top rows in the collection boxes. Every jar in my mother's kitchen has airholes in the top—she's stopped putting anything in them that can leak.

I have my own collection—bugs I've caught and others I got through catalogs. Even though the exotic ones are fun, there's nothing like going out in my backyard or Suzanne's and finding something that I've always wanted to find. I spend a lot of time looking in buckets of standing water, picking up big rocks, and kneeling in fields of goldenrod. My personal favorites are beetles—all different kinds—bombardier, stag, ladybird, tiger. . . .

Which reminds me that my friend Heidi, who's a real entomologist at the university, will be bringing a special beetle to our school Monday for the Insect Fair. She lets me watch in her laboratory where she does research on hissing cockroaches; I even get to hold them and hear them hiss. Okay, it might not be an activity for everyone, but in my book, it's tops.

I'm planning on bringing my collection tomorrow, along with my bug jars. Mrs. Greene lets me bring in any bug I find provided we keep it in a glass jar and eventually let it go. She wants everything to be educational so I tell the other kids what to feed each bug

9

and how to handle it. I've even been called to other classes in my role as unofficial "bug buster." A substitute in Mr. Carleton's class opened her lunch bag one day and started screaming that there was "an enormous creature" on her blueberry yogurt container. None of the other teachers would take a look so they called me. I opened the bag only to discover a poor, terrified silverfish (who was a bit on the large side). When I picked him up to let him go, some of the teachers backed away and said, "Eeeww!"

Bugs get a bad rap. So my goal in life is to try to make people, if not *love* bugs, at least like them a little. I know that if I were a bug, I sure wouldn't want everyone looking at me saying, "Eeeww!" all the time.

A Piece of Junk

I thought about the walking stick as I was getting ready for bed that night. When the bell for recess rang and the rest of us were filing in, Suzanne had run back to the insect and put it in an empty corn chips bag. She was worried, too, that the walking stick would get smashed. I would have taken it except for my recent visit to the principal's office. I knew also that Suzanne had wanted a walking stick for her bug collection for a long time. I'll bet her new best friends haven't seen that.

After school I asked her if I could see the walking stick but she said no, that it was in her backpack and she was in a hurry (to catch up with the sissy girls). Then, to top it off, when I walked past her house later, she was sitting alone on her front porch giggling about something. But she wouldn't tell me why.

Girls.

Even the most normal ones get goofy.

I looked around for Spidey, the little cobweb spider that lived in my room. There he was, weaving a web in his favorite spot, on top of my desk lamp. I know a ton about spiders.

Spiders are not insects because insects always have six legs. Spiders belong to a group of animals called arachnids. Arachnids have no antennae or wings and have eight legs. Cobweb spiders live outdoors and in basements of houses, which is where I found Spidey. Even though he looks wimpy, Spidey, like all spiders, has poison in his fangs. On a cobweb spider it's a small amount, but it's the poison that hurts when you get a spider bite. Spidey's special superpower is his web: Cobweb spiders' webs are so strong and well designed that they can actually

trap small snakes and mice, not to mention most insects.

Spidey scurried down from the wall. I opened my hand and he crawled right into my palm. I petted his little brown back then I put him down on my desk since he likes the bright light. We were just sitting together when there was a knock on my door. It had to be one of my parents since my sister can't read yet—even though the extremely large KNOCK sign was made especially for her. My mom stuck her head inside the door.

"Hi, Mom."

"Hi, honey." She was squinting suspiciously at my hand on the desk. She sometimes needs preparation for my newest bug-jar residents. I opened my palm to show her it was just Spidey. She smiled and handed me a small package. "This is for you."

It was wrapped in plain brown paper. On the front were the words: FOR THE WORLD'S GREATEST BUG BOY."

"Who's it from?" I said, turning it over.

She shrugged her shoulders. "I don't know. It was on the front step when I let the cat in."

Now she stepped inside and did her nightly "smell check." Since we disagree on how often my room needs cleaning, my mom said that if she smelled any "science projects," it was time.

But this time she didn't say anything. Whew!

"It's time for bed, Charlie. Get in your pajamas and you can read until nine." Bending over, she kissed the top of my head.

"Okay, Mom. Good night."

As soon as she shut the door, I grabbed the scissors from my desk drawer and tore the paper off the package. I held up a sheet of cardboard with a plastic tube stuck to it. It was so dusty I had to wipe it on my jeans before I could read the words across the top: THE AMAZING BUG-A-VIEW!

What? Was this a joke? This thing looked like it was a hundred years old.

On the sides of the cardboard were these words: ASTOUND YOUR FRIENDS! LEARN THE SECRETS OF THE ANCIENTS! A MUST-HAVE TOOL FOR ANY SERIOUS BUG COLLECTOR!

Oh, sure. I turned over the cardboard, looking for a name, the person who'd take credit for this package. Zippo. All I could see was TAKES TWO AAA BATTERIES.

I took the Bug-A-View off the cardboard. It looked like a flashlight except that there was a small hole at the top to look through to the bottom. I looked through it at a pencil on my desk. The pencil was slightly enlarged. Oh, so that's the Amazing Bug-A-View! A flashlight with a hole through it and a lousy magnifying glass at the end.

Just for the heck of it I opened my bottom desk drawer, pulled out two batteries, and popped them in. Then I noticed a small red button on the side. I pushed it. When I looked through the hole now, the pencil was lit up a little. Gee, how amazing. I noticed that around the small red button were some words: SEE THE WORLD FROM A BUG'S-EYE VIEW!

I laughed out loud with that one. This piece of junk was worse than the stuff my sister gets at the drive-up window at Burger Blastoff.

I tossed the "must-have tool" onto my desk. It was late; I needed to go to bed. Picking up my book,

Huggable Buggies, I looked around for Spidey only to find that he had crawled onto the magnifying end of the Bug-A-View.

As I searched through clothing piles on the floor for my pajamas, I glanced back up at the Bug-A-View. I'd left the light on.

Spidey was still there.

What did he like about it so much?

I sat down at my desk and leaned forward to look at the bottom of the magnifier. Spidey's little body made a dark outline against the light. As I watched him, the light inside seemed to get stronger and brighter. My eyes started to water.

And then Spidey disappeared.

Eight-Legged Cat Dessert

I opened my eyes. I guess I'd fallen asleep. But now I didn't know where I was. I had a very strange feeling—like something was wrong. Very wrong.

My body tingled all over, like that numb, prickly feeling you get when your arm or leg falls asleep. I also felt light, almost weightless, as if my limbs weren't connected to the rest of my body.

And now I realized where I was—on top of my desk. But my eyes didn't seem to be working right because my room and everything in it was gigantic and at strange angles. I could see everything in my room—the bed, dresser, door, window—all at the same time, without moving my head.

I was in a path of bright light. It was coming from a large shape next to me that looked familiar. And then I realized what it was: the Bug-A-View. I went to pick it up. But then I stopped.

Because I had no arms.

Or hands.

But I had something. I tried to look at my arms but my eyes wouldn't focus down. I tried to feel my legs. They didn't feel like my legs. I lifted one high enough to see.

Yaaa!

My leg. It was gone. There was just a tiny, shriveled, hairy twig in its place! And there was more than one. More than two.

These legs, this body—they didn't belong to me. They belonged to somebody else. Somebody I knew very well. Somebody who could have been in my insect collection. Somebody like . . . SPIDEY!

I had turned into Spidey.

I took a step forward, pulling half of my legs with me.

The other four weren't moving. Hmmm. I could see that it was hard to get all your legs working together when you have eight of them. I tried to concentrate, to move them all sideways at the same time. Here we go, nice and WHOA!

I jerked hard to one side, careening wildly. My little spider body could hardly keep up with my legs, which were moving incredibly fast and felt out of control. I tumbled backward off the edge of my desk.

I braced myself to hit the floor.

But wait a minute.

I was on the underside of my desk. I forgot that spiders don't have to jump, they can crawl around the edge and go down the side. What a dummy!

I started moving downward. These legs were working better now. Wow! I was zooming along.

I reached a jungle of tall, upright brown stuff—my thick carpeting. I could barely move in it. My legs kept sinking. I had to scale each fiber like a mountain climber.

But wait a minute. Spiders don't have to crawl on the carpeting.

I crawled over to the nearest wall and started to climb. I remembered that a spider's eight eyes are placed around its head and work independently of each other. They move up and down and swivel around. I was starting to get the feel of them.

Cool! I could really zip across the wall. It was like a superfast roller-coaster ride. Up and down I zigzagged, reaching the hallway in no time.

The hallway from my room to my parents' room was not very wide. I once counted how many steps it took me to cross it—about three giant ones. But from my present shrunken state, the hallway looked like a cavernous tunnel. I decided to go for it anyway.

Whoosh! Was I making time. I breezed across that hallway faster than it took me to walk. I did a long jump from the doorway to my parents' bed and landed on one of the bedposts. Clambering down onto the bedspread, I almost sank into the squishy material. But quick as a flash I was up and skimming over the surface.

I reached what I thought was my mother's arm lying on top of the bedspread. I was faced with an important decision—what's the best way to wake her up and minimize my chances of getting squashed? I hadn't yet thought of the way I was going to communicate to her that this little brown eight-legged creepy-crawly was her adorable son, Charlie.

Cautiously, I started up her arm.

WHOOSH!

It was an earthquake! No! A tornado!

I dug my legs in and held on for life. It felt like an enormously strong wind was trying to sweep me away.

Then it was calm and quiet.

But soon enough the tornado started again. I realized what was happening—my mother was breathing! As I crawled up onto her shoulder, she inhaled.

YAHHH!

I lost my balance and slid down the side of her neck.

21

I started to climb up again, holding tight with my legs. I must have reached her cheek.

Well, I thought, catching my breath, I can't get much closer than this.

"Mom," I whispered. "It's me, Charlie. Your son."

Nothing happened. What the heck am I whispering for?

"MMMMMOOOOOOOMMMMMMM!!!!"

I know, I know. This is stupid beyond belief. Of course, no sound came out of my pathetic little body.

I forgot about that.

WHOA!

The tornado again! More powerful than ever. It was like a gigantic vacuum, trying to suck me up. I grasped as hard as I could, struggling to stay where I was. I could see four of my legs dangling in the wind. And then, there was a deafening roar.

It's a snore! HELP! I'm going to be inhaled by my own mother!

The vacuum suddenly reversed and I was thrown forward into the air with tremendous force. Soaring out of my parents' room, I finally crash-landed in the hallway.

My head was spinning. My eyes were crisscrossed all over the place. My legs were tangled together. Where was I? I could make out a bright light behind me. It was low, not high in the ceiling. I must be near the night-light that we keep on for Lucy, my sister.

Suddenly my body started vibrating wildly. What was going on? The fine hairs on my legs were tingling and prickly, like super-goose bumps. There was *something* that my body was trying to tell me.

ALERT! ALERT!

Now I knew what it was—my spider sense warning me about some danger nearby. The problem was I didn't know if I could make sense out of what my senses were telling me.

Aha! The danger was in the form of the feline couch potato, my yellow tabby cat, Blanche. She was in the doorway to my room, staring steadily at me, her long tail twitching with excitement. Her yellow eyes (which were closed 90 percent of the time) were boring into my small body, waiting . . . waiting . . . to pounce.

Oh no! Was I going to end up as cat dessert?

Blanche took a step closer. With one eye, I looked behind me for someplace to hide. But then I noticed something—the back of my spider body. A large bump with holes in it. In other words, my abdomen and my . . . SPIN-NERETS.

Whoosh! I shot out a long line of silk. Blanche's whiskers were suddenly covered with a thin white veil. She brought her paws together in front of her face, trying to brush it away. The silk lines were barely visible but I knew how strong and sticky they were.

Then I remembered my other superarachnid trait, specifically the one that helps spiders even the score against larger animals—my fangs.

I was suddenly dying to try them out. I crept closer to Blanche who was still batting herself in the face. I poised myself directly above her tail. I could get a good, meaty bite of it.

I raised my fangs, ready to strike.

Then I lowered my fangs. I couldn't do it, not to poor, unsuspecting Blanche. She's a good cat, just following her instincts. (Now I knew exactly how that felt!) I knew what a spider bite would do to a human, but not to a cat. I would feel bad if she got sick.

And speaking of feeling bad, my mom was going to feel pretty bad if she discovered that her son had turned into a

creepy-crawly overnight. Even worse if she smashed me with a newspaper. She was more open to bugs than she used to be, but I think this would be stretching it.

I crawled back quickly into my room and climbed to the top of my desk. The light from the Bug-A-View was still on. I made my way onto the glass at the end of the magnifier, the way I remembered last seeing Spidey's body.

The light grew stronger; the glass began to get hot. My body was tingling. I closed my eight eyes and hoped when I opened them again, I'd have only two.

Do the Hop

"**M**om! Charlie's eating his cereal with a fork!"

Lucy's screech jolted me out of the twilight zone. It was Saturday morning and I was tired. Very tired. I looked down at the fork I was holding; no wonder my Rice Crispies tasted . . . pointy.

"Charlie," my mom's voice echoed Lucy's, "what is the matter with you lately? You've got bugs on the brain. At school you're sent to the principal; at home you're practically asleep in your cereal bowl. It's time to straighten up."

I threw down my fork. Pain-In, again. It's the only way she could have known about my visit to the principal's office. Mr. Baxter said he wouldn't call my parents.

"Can't a guy eat his Rice Crispies with a fork if he

wants to?" I stood up and dramatically threw my napkin on top of my fork. "I need some privacy."

I heard my mom whispering to Lucy to leave me alone as I stalked out of the kitchen. Climbing up the stairs, I stood outside the door to my bedroom for a minute before entering. My heart was pounding. I had to face the Bug-A-View and think about last night's events.

When I woke up this morning, I had my doubts that anything really happened. Just a nasty dream from unknowingly eating three slices of tofu pizza at dinner last night. (Mom told us it was tofu *after* we'd finished eating.)

And then I saw the Bug-A-View on my desk. The light was still on.

Details of the past night came back to me. I remembered being able to see in front of me and in back of me at the same time. Trying to move my eight legs. Flinging out my spinnerets.

But how did I know for real that it had all happened? I mean, just because a guy wakes up naked in bed doesn't necessarily mean that he turned into his pet cobweb spider, does it?

Then I saw something at the foot of my bed. Something that would prove if what I thought happened last night really occurred.

Blanche the cat—archenemy of cobweb spiders.

I lifted her head.

Two strings of silk dangled from her whiskers.

On wobbly legs, I walked all the way around my desk. From a far corner, I reached over and carefully

pushed the button on the Bug-A-View, steering very clear of the beam of light. I read the little words again: SEE THE WORLD FROM A BUG'S-EYE VIEW!

Funny. Very funny.

And now what do I do? Tell my mom? Call Heidi? I lay down on my bed and gazed up. In the farthest corner of my ceiling, I could see Spidey back in his usual spot. He was probably pretty zonked out, too. Suddenly I knew exactly what to do. I grabbed the Bug-A-View, bounded down the stairs and out of the house.

I had to show it to Suzanne. Maybe we could even try it together.

Passing by the Wintertrees', I could see Raymond sitting at the piano, practicing his scales. He saw me and stopped playing. I could tell that he wanted to wave or say "Hi," which I usually do, but today I just gave him a dirty look and kept going. Besides, I didn't want him to see the Bug-A-View.

I was out of breath by the time I pushed Suzanne's doorbell. During the summer Suzanne and I used to watch *Spiderman* together on Saturday mornings and then go for a bug hunt. But we hadn't done that since school started. No one was coming to the door. I pushed the bell again, knocked, and waited. I was getting impatient.

I knocked again really hard and then almost fell on top of Mrs. Dimarian when she opened the door.

"Charlie! Is something wrong?" She looked alarmed.

"No," I answered quickly. "Is Suzanne home?"

She shook her head. "I'm afraid not. She left a few minutes ago with the girls." We both knew which girls, of course. I turned away angrily and started walking away.

"Is there something I can do for you, Charlie?" Mrs. Dimarian asked from the door. She knew I was upset. I shook my head.

"I'll tell Suzanne you were here," she shouted and waved good-bye at me. I waved back so she didn't get worried and call my mom.

I didn't watch where I was going and tripped over a stone, dropping the Bug-A-View on someone's lawn. As I bent over to get it I realized the button was pushed in. It must have happened when the Bug-A-View fell.

I noticed some movement on a big tree next to me and turned to look. It was a huge brown grasshopper. Without thinking, I raised the Bug-A-View to my eye for a better look and YIPES!

There I was on the tree. Hanging on for dear life. Because . . . you guessed it.

I was now perched on gray, bumpy bark that was tricky to hang on to—if you're not used to being a grasshopper, that is.

Shuffling my hind legs around, I dug in for a steadier foothold. I knew that grasshoppers' enormous folding legs move so fast and jump so far that I needed to be careful. I had to get down the tree to get to the Bug-A-View. Unfolding my right hind leg, I began to—*whoa!*

Suddenly I was soaring high through the air and then dropping down, fast. Oh no. I was going to crash. Watch out!

My legs extended all the way out and I landed gently on something green and tickly. Grass, I figured, although from my perspective it was more like a forest. I had no idea where the Bug-A-View was. Then, to top it off, I suddenly had an overwhelming urge to . . . rub. Rub? And here I go, rub, rub, rubbing my hind legs together.

CHIRP!

What? What was that? A sound. A loud sound. And it came from a strange place on my body.

CHIRP!

Then I remembered: grasshoppers are related to crickets and katydids. They all chirp when they rub their legs together. Their eardrums are near where their hind legs connect with their abdomens.

But I still needed to find out where I was and the only way to do that was to hop around. I took a deep breath, arranged my legs, and *WHOOSH!* shot off like a rocket through the air.

Wow! This was fun.

I landed on something harder than grass. The sidewalk.

My eyes didn't see too well but I thought I could make out the Dimarians' mailbox, which sat on the sidewalk in front of their house. It was bright yellow with big purple polka dots. I was pretty sure that the Bug-A-View was near the tree in their neighbors' front yard. If I could steer my legs in the right direction I should be able to get pretty close.

I took off again, propelling myself at a slight angle toward where I thought I should go. Soaring up so fast and hard was an incredible feeling—like swinging really high on a swing and then letting go and pushing off through the air.

Whew! I did it. I landed pretty close to the tree. Now that I was getting used to my legs I could stand up a little and not take off. I looked around and spotted the Bug-A-View a short distance away.

Being an experienced grasshopper by now, I did a perfect little hop over to it. Leaping up gracefully, I landed right on top of the glass. The light was beaming.

And then I was back, sitting on top of the Bug-A-View in Suzanne's neighbor's front yard.

I looked down; everything seemed to be okay. Better than okay, in fact. I felt great. Like a million bucks. I had just turned into a grasshopper, and now, instantly, I was back to myself. I could do it anytime I wanted, anywhere I wanted. And I could choose whatever bug I wanted to become. I'd be the next Spiderman, or Grasshopperman, for that matter.

I gazed at the Bug-A-View in my hand.

The possibilities were limitless.

Buzz Off

Walking slowly down the sidewalk, I thought about transforming into my favorite insects. An assassin bug. A walking stick. A leaf-cutter ant. A rhinoceros beetle. A black widow spider. I knew now that the Bug-A-View worked like a charm; transforming back and forth was as easy as pie.

I was now almost glad that Suzanne hadn't been home. I didn't know if I wanted to share the Bug-A-View with her or anyone, for that matter. Which reminded me: Who knew about the Bug-A-View? And more important, who gave it to me?

Even though it was a beautiful Saturday morning, there was no one outside on the block. That was lucky for me since I hadn't exactly planned to turn into a grasshopper. Next time, I'd have to be more careful.

Next time!

I was already thinking ahead.

I heard some piano music and realized that I was near the Wintertrees' house. Raymond was still at his lesson. I put my head down, ready to pass by quickly. But then I stopped dead in my tracks. An idea was forming inside my head. A brilliant idea.

I could bug Raymond.

Not in the way that he bugs me at school by trying to get me, and everyone else in trouble. Not that way.

No, I mean *really* bug Raymond.

By becoming a bug. The buggiest kind of bug.

I dashed around the side of the Wintertrees' house to search for the garbage cans. Where were they? In the garage, I remembered. Shielding my eyes, I peered into the small rectangular window on the garage door. Inside, I could make out two large, dark green garbage cans. I found a small side door and slipped inside.

The lids on the garbage cans were not on very tight. I grabbed one, yanked it off, and finally found what I had been searching for—a fly.

A big, black, ugly, noisy fly, hovering over some cantaloupe rinds. Perfect. I brushed at the fly and got him outside.

Suddenly I heard a loud noise. The garage door! It

was going up! No time to lose. I aimed the Bug-A-View, pressed the button, and . . .

BUZZ! Say hello to Charlie Kaplan, the new fly on the block. And boy, can flies fly! I circled the entire garage in a split second. Then I did it again, even faster.

What speed. What agility.

What a cinch!

Now that I was one of the fastest flying insects alive I whizzed above the garbage cans, tempted to check out those cantaloupe rinds; they smelled delicious. But I was soaring so high and so fast that I didn't want to stop. Ever. As I circled at breakneck speed around the garage I could make out some movement and noise. I paused for an instant; it was Mr. Wintertree, whistling as he puttered around. But I couldn't stop to watch because I was a fly with a mission.

I flew around to the front of the house and landed on the windowsill. My powerful wings helped to keep me on a steady course so I wouldn't take a sudden nosedive into the side of the house. Raymond was practicing his lessons on the piano. I wedged myself through a small hole in the screen and waited while he paused to look at something in his music. Then he started up again.

This was it. Payback time.

I flew up around his face slowly. Hmmm. Where do I begin? Where would be the most irritating place to begin my buzzing? His ears, of course. I raced around to the back of

his head, and started going in small fast circles from one ear to the other and over again. He jerked his head over to his right shoulder then to his left, then to his right, then to his left, faster and faster.

Landing lightly on his left ear I could see that Raymond had a few freckles. Awww, aren't those cute? I'll tickle them a little. Let's see how much earwax he has.

Hey! Watch it! A large light-colored thing with moving parts loomed up to hit me but missed. It was his hand.

Okay, Raymond. You asked for it.

I zoomed around the front of his head and made a beeline, landing on the tip of his nose. My compound eye was made up of thousands of lenses; I could see from every possible angle. That's what makes flies so hard to catch; they see you coming from a mile away. And from one of my farthest lenses I could make out a moving . . .

"Owww!"

I'd zoomed away just in time for Raymond to smack himself on the nose. Hah! Take that!

Flying away for a moment, I would let him think that he had gotten rid of me. It worked; he started playing again. I coasted above his head for a bit then shot down, like a rocket, in front of his face. He swatted, but he was way off.

Missed me, missed me, now ya gotta kiss me.

Now I was darting in and out of his fingers on the piano keys. On top, then underneath, in and around, I did a classic figure eight up to his face and then down again, with a little hide-and-seek under his hand. He was swatting everywhere, muttering under his breath and trying to keep playing. I was getting a bit bored with this, so I paused for a moment, to think about my next plan of attack.

CRASH!

I felt a sudden burst of air and flew upward. What was that? It sounded like a thunderous wave crashing into some

rocks. I saw that the piano keys had disappeared. Then I knew: Raymond had slammed the piano shut. He was trying to flatten me!

SMASH!

Now he's trying to swat me in midair. I zoomed up to the top of his head and dived into his hair. But he suddenly reached up and started swatting again. This was getting tricky.

A voice called from outside. "When you're done with your practicing, Raymond, you can clip the grass near the front porch."

"Okay," Raymond replied. As I rested on his piano bench and plotted my next move I was troubled by a niggling thought. It was what Raymond's father had just said; there was something wrong with it.

Thud! Raymond's hand smashed down and almost got me that time. I wasn't paying enough attention to him because I now knew what was troubling me: a sound. A motorized sound that was coming from outside the window. The lawnmower. Raymond's father was mowing the lawn. And now I realized that the sound had been going on for a while. But why should that bother me?

I flew over to the windowsill to think. Why would it be bad that Raymond's father was mowing the lawn? And then I had it: the Bug-A-View! Where did I leave it? In the garage? Outside? On the lawn?

I couldn't remember!

I flew out the window to retrace my route. Okay.

First, I'd gone into the garage. Opened the lid of the garbage can. Found the fly. Then what? I chased the fly outside to the backyard. Then I heard Mr. Wintertree open the garage door. The Bug-A-View must be on the grass in the yard.

I zoomed around the side of the garage to find it. But there was nothing there. I slowed down to search; I didn't see anything. Which meant that Mr. Wintertree must have already mowed the backyard and moved the Bug-A-View! To where? Would he have thrown it in the garbage? I zoomed back into the garage.

It had to be in here. If my dad had found something on the grass he would have thrown it in the garbage. Right? But where were the garbage cans? They were gone!

Oh no.

Without the Bug-A-View I would have to remain a . . . a . . . no, I couldn't even *think* it. I had to find the garbage can.

Then I smelled something. Something that I had smelled not too long ago. Cantaloupe. Cantaloupe rinds, to be exact. I followed the smell out the garage door, down the driveway to the street curb. Today was garbage day and Mr. Wintertree had moved them out there for pickup. I flew over.

The cans were empty!

Flying down the block, I easily caught up with the garbage truck and dove into the freshly dumped trash. I was plunged into stinky darkness. Now the truck was slowing down. In a second the garbagemen would be dumping more

garbage on top of the Wintertrees'. I must find the Bug-A-View, fast!

Suddenly, I saw a beam of light and before I knew it I was blinded by the glass.

"Hey! What the heck's going on here?"

Two garbagemen were staring at me. I must be a boy again because they sure wouldn't notice a fly. I tried to get up but there was too much stuff on top of me. Stuff, as in eggshells and baked beans and dirty paper towels and rumpled tissues and coffee

grounds and old baloney and half-eaten pizza slices
and—well, you get the picture.

"I, I . . ."

I had to go with the I'm-just-a-stupid-kid excuse;
there was no alternative under the circumstances. I
shrugged, smiled, and looked blank.

They each grabbed an arm and hauled me up,
muttering and shaking their heads. When the truck
pulled away, I was practically in front of my house.

I looked down and realized that I was holding the
Bug-A-View, which was covered with tomato sauce.

"Hey!" I shouted at the garbage truck. "I have something else to throw in there!"

But it was too late; they were rounding the corner. I didn't want the Bug-A-View anymore, not any part of it. Ever again. When I thought of how easily I could've missed the garbage truck and still be buzzing above stinky garbage cans, waiting to get splattered, well, a cold shiver ran down my spine—either that or it was some Jell-O.

I was so glad to be home I even got a little choked up as I opened the back door. I stuck the Bug-A-View in my back pocket and ran into the bathroom to clean up before my mom saw me. I'd throw it out later.

From now on, Bug Boy is just sticking to the "boy" part.

Manny's Crunchy Snack

"Poor Manny," Suzanne said, her nose pressed to the glass jar. "He finished all his ants already."

On Monday the Insect Fair was in progress. Suzanne and I were in our classroom, watching Manny, the six-inch-long praying mantis I'd caught behind my grandmother's garage the other day. I'd only caught Manny to display at the fair today. It's important not to catch and keep praying mantises because they help the environment by eating bugs like fruit flies, which destroy crops.

I shifted my gaze to the coatrack, making sure, for the one-thousandth time today, that my backpack was still hanging there. Inside my backpack were Spidey (in his jar) and the Bug-A-View. I know, I know, I never wanted to see the darned thing again. But let me explain.

After a long shower and a good night's sleep, I felt back to normal. My two transformations seemed like dreams (or nightmares) by now. But when I was ready to leave this morning, I found Lucy playing with some stuff in my closet. And guess where I had put the Bug-A-View? Suddenly I pictured coming home from school and finding a millipede lying on Lucy's pillow and no Lucy around. So I figured the Bug-A-View was safer with me.

Suzanne was cleaning some old twigs out of Manny's box. I realized that this was the first time in a long while that Suzanne and I were bug watching together. I leaned down next to her and watched Manny rub his front legs together. This gesture is what makes the mantis look as if he's praying, which is how he got his name. Those legs or "arms" on the mantis are incredibly fast and powerful so he can catch a lot of live food, which he does almost constantly for the several months he's alive.

I was a little worried about Manny because all I'd been able to find for him were some small brown ants, which weren't nearly enough for the "insect cannibals," as praying mantises are otherwise known. Heidi said that she'd bring Manny a surprise treat today.

And now Suzanne was asking me something about the other night. Even though I missed it, I knew that she'd asked me the same question a

moment before. I shook my head, hoping *no* was a sane response.

She scrunched up her face at me. "What's wrong with you today? Didn't you sleep enough last night?"

I shrugged my shoulders.

"I thought you might have something else to show at the Insect Fair," she said, still looking puzzled.

I was about to remind her that my insect collection was displayed in another room. Since this was an all-school event, there were exhibits in all the different classrooms. But then Mrs. Greene clapped her hands for attention. Pain-In started "SSSHing" everyone, reminding me of how perfect his nickname fit him and how much fun I'd had "bugging" him, at first, at least.

"Kids! Our visitor has arrived," announced Mrs. Greene.

Heidi stepped into the classroom, lugging her usual stuff. She waved to the kids and winked at me.

"Boys and girls, please welcome Professor Heidi MacIntosh, an entomologist from the university who's going to show us some insects that we hope don't get loose." Mrs. Greene smiled with concern.

Everybody laughed. Heidi looked the way she usually did, which wasn't exactly how you'd think a "bug scientist" should look. Today she wore a wide, beige cowboy hat that had fringe on it and one of those funny skinny ties around her neck, with a silver Goliath beetle clip to hold it together. Suzanne nudged me again and pointed to Heidi's red cowboy boots. Since Heidi wears what *she* wants, I figured that when I become a famous entomologist I'd be able to wear my glow-in-the-dark spider T-shirt every day.

"Okay, you guys," Heidi said, with a sly smile. "You are in for a major, humongous, awesome, totally B-A-D surprise today."

Suzanne shouted "Wooo!"

Danny yelled, "All right!"

Heidi walked over to the display table, which was next to the sink at the back of the room. She took out

a terrarium, a large glass jar, and a smaller jar. I squinted to see what was inside the small jar; from where I sat it looked like an ordinary pill bug or millipede.

Unless it's a . . .

I moved closer for a better look.

Wow!

A bombardier beetle! I couldn't believe it.

I looked up excitedly. Heidi was watching me, a huge smile on her face. "I thought you might like this one, Bug Boy."

An average person would barely notice a bombardier beetle; they are small, brown, and ordinary looking. (I think of them as the Clark Kent of beetles.) But bombardiers have an extra-special superpower: when attacked, they spray their enemies with a "bomb" of hot chemicals that explode from their rear ends, with a *pop*. It usually doesn't kill an insect, but I don't think many stick around to find out for sure. Heidi, who likes beetles a lot, too, knew that I'd always wanted to see one. Maybe I'd get to hold it and feel its spray.

There was an extremely large, black, hairy female tarantula in the terrarium. For a second I got scared—having just had firsthand experience with spider sense—that the tarantula would think that there was an overgrown boy-sized arachnid and shoot out its venom at me. But I realized that I was

just panicking. I knew that tarantulas only attack when they feel threatened, and as Charlie Kaplan I was pretty harmless. I glanced over at my backpack to make sure it was still safe.

In the large glass jar was a rust-colored, almond-shaped Giant Cockroach. Heidi liked to bring this to show people that close up, cockroaches were harmless and even sort of pretty.

Right now Heidi was talking about tarantulas, stuff I already knew. She pointed to Danny, who had his hand up.

"If a spider bites you, can you ever get special spider powers?"

I waited for the class to laugh. But hardly anyone did. They were all waiting to hear if they should risk a bite to become Spiderman.

Heidi laughed. "Well, I haven't heard that happening to anyone since Peter Parker spilled radioactive chemicals on the spider in his lab. But spider bites can hurt, because their fangs contain poison."

"Don't some centipedes have poison in their bites, too?" asked Suzanne.

Heidi nodded. "Yep, that's right. If a desert centipede bites you, you can get pretty sick."

"I wonder why there's not a Centipedeman?" Danny wondered.

"Too many legs," said Heidi and I at the same time.

Everyone laughed.

"Centipedes are creepy," said Raymond. I noticed he had finished drawing an "I love Heidi" picture, with a you-know-what for the *love*.

Mrs. Greene walked to the front of the room. "Heidi is due to give a talk with some slides of her research to the whole school in the gym after recess, in about an hour. And in honor of the Insect Fair, today at recess you are all going to learn how to dance the tarantella."

Kids were now gathering around the display table. I could see Suzanne holding the giant cock-

roach; Danny was letting the tarantula climb up his arm. I hurried to the table to get my chance to hold the bombardier. Heidi was rummaging around in her bags. I heard her muttering to herself.

"What's the matter?" I asked her.

"I forgot my slides for the talk. What a dummy!" She smacked her head with her hand. Heidi was the only grown-up I knew who forgot stuff all the time, like me. I think she had what my mom called "bugs on the brain." That was another thing I liked about her.

"I'm going to have to run back to the lab to get my stuff," Heidi explained. "Since I'm not due to talk for a little while I think I can make it in time." She began to pack up her insect gear.

"Aw, do you have to take these guys?" Suzanne now had the tarantula on her shoulder.

"We'll watch them," I joined in. "You know that I can take care of them for a little while."

Heidi looked at us, trying to decide. "Okay, I guess you can be a bug-sitter for a little while, Charlie." Her face got serious. "But I don't want anyone handling them while I'm gone."

"Okay," I replied. That seemed fine. Just spending more time with the bugs was a treat.

Heidi waved good-bye and zipped out the door. A second later she rushed back in holding a large plastic bag. "I forgot to leave this! Could somebody grab it?"

Raymond rushed up to get the bag. He's always the first one to help the teacher—or any other adult in the classroom. I had a feeling that this time he might just regret it. Heidi handed the bag to him and left.

Raymond looked down at it.

I put my fingers in my ears.

Clark Kent Escapes

"**E**EEEEKKKK!!!!"

Raymond let out a sonar-level scream and dropped the bag. About twenty little brown crickets scrambled all over the floor. It was Manny's surprise treat.

"Raymond!" yelled Mrs. Greene.

The whole class dropped to their knees and started trying to pick up the crickets (except Raymond, of course, who was standing on the seat of his desk, whimpering). Suzanne scooped a handful that were running toward the door. Another girl was on her stomach, trying to grab a few that ran under the teacher's desk. Danny had a broom and was sweeping them toward another boy who was holding a dustpan. Mrs. Greene looked like she wanted to join

Raymond on top of the seat but couldn't because she was the teacher.

Amazingly, we seemed to find most of the crickets. I took the lid off of Manny's jar and dumped the crickets inside; Manny looked very excited about his new food. We all stood around and watched him catch his lunch.

Suddenly there was a gasp from the back of the room.

"Oh no!"

I turned around. Suzanne was at the display table pointing at something.

"It's gone!"

Gone? What's gone? I raced over to the table.

The lid on the bombardier beetle's jar was not on all the way.

I stared at it, dumbfounded, my brain not accepting what my eyes were seeing. The jar was empty. Completely bare. I quickly checked the other insects; their containers were secure.

But the beetle was gone.

"Oh, no." I closed my eyes. I couldn't believe this was happening. Here I'd just told Heidi that I could take care of the bugs, and ten minutes after she's gone, one was missing.

It had to be around somewhere. How well could it hide?

Pretty darned well, I discovered. As Suzanne

and I started tearing the display table apart and searching under everything, I remembered the most basic insect superpower: camouflage. The Clark Kent of beetles, I knew, was particularly easy to overlook. Danny was crawling around on the floor nearby. Mrs. Greene (who seemed sort of dazed by now) and some other kids came over.

"How did this happen?" she asked, looking sternly at me. "Didn't you put the beetle back in his jar and screw the lid on tightly?"

The answer, of course, was no. When Heidi left, I was holding the beetle. Then Raymond dropped the crickets, and I quickly grabbed the glass jar and put the beetle back inside. Since I was in a hurry, I didn't put the lid on all the way.

I didn't have an excuse and Mrs. Greene knew it. "I think another visit to Mr. Baxter's office might be in order, Charlie. I just don't know what's gotten into you," she said angrily. "And this time I'll tell him to call your parents."

This is Pain-In's fault! I wanted to scream at her. He's done it again. If he hadn't been such a baby and dropped the crickets none of this would have happened. But I didn't say it. I knew that it was my fault for not closing the jar tight enough no matter how stupid Raymond had acted.

Bending over, I continued searching the floor.

Where could the beetle be? It was as if he'd disappeared into thin air. Then I realized that if the beetle
was on the floor, he might get stepped on! What was
I going to tell Heidi? I glanced at the clock. Luckily,
recess was in five minutes so everyone would leave
the room. But that also meant that Heidi would be
back soon.

If only I was Spiderman, I'd be able to find the
beetle with my spider sense. Because spider sense
alerts spiders to any dangerous insects nearby. It also
helps the spider find insects to eat that it can trap in
its web such as gnats, flies . . . or beetles.

I sat up straight. I'm not really thinking what I
think I'm thinking, I thought.

Am I?

Beetles. Spider sense. Spidey. The Bug-A-View.

Oh, no. Not after I almost became a permanent member of the fly community.

I can't use the Bug-A-View again, can I?

I took a deep breath. Well, if I am extra careful about where I leave the Bug-A-View, which just happens to be in my backpack along with Spidey.

Besides, even if I don't use it, I still have to see Mr. Baxter, who will have to see my parents, who will definitely punish me.

Mrs. Greene's voice shook me out of my plans. "Charlie Kaplan!" The class was lining up at the door.

Suzanne grabbed my arm. "Charlie, let's ask her if we can skip recess and look for the beetle."

"Um-um-no, Suzanne," I stammered, lowering my voice. "You go, be on the lookout for Heidi. If you see her, stall her."

Suzanne nodded gravely, understanding the importance of the situation. At least she was loyal at a time like this.

My mind was racing. *I'm going to do it.* But could I transform, come back to the classroom, find the beetle, and transform back in thirty minutes?

"Mrs. Greene," I said as the last of the kids left. "I'm going to get a flashlight and some other stuff to find the beetle."

She nodded. "When you find it, cap it tightly, and then join the class in the gym."

I casually unhooked my backpack, waved good-bye to Mrs. Greene, and strolled out the door. Once in the hallway, I looked around frantically. I needed a safe place to transform. It was too dangerous to stay in the classroom; kids always ran back to get their mitts or balls.

Then I thought of a good place: the older boys' bathroom, on the other side of the building. It was too risky to use the bathroom near our room. I took the longer route to the bathroom; through the gym is a shortcut, but I certainly didn't want to see anyone in my class, or worse, Heidi.

My stomach had gone beyond feeling bad; now it was doing cartwheels and somersaults. I closed my eyes and pushed the bathroom door.

Spidey at School

Slipping inside the bathroom, I leaned against the wall and took a deep breath. Yuck! It smelled terrible. I ran into the farthest stall. As I closed the door I could hear a group of boys come in. Great.

I tried to make as little noise as possible as I unzipped my backpack and took out Spidey and the Bug-A-View. I looked around for a place to put them. I didn't want to put them on the floor, then anyone could bend down and see them. So I stood, facing the back wall so that my feet would look normal if someone glanced underneath. I waited for the boys to leave. But they didn't. They were having a spitting contest from the first stall into the sinks under the mirrors. I looked up at the clock. Four minutes of recess gone already.

I couldn't wait any longer for them to leave. Flushing the toilet, I strolled out of the stall. One of the older boys stopped spitting to stare at me.

"Hey, what's a runt like you doing in our bathroom?"

The other boys laughed. I made what I hoped were some convincing laugh sounds so that it seemed like I was laughing at myself too. Yeah, sure, guys, that's pretty funny.

"Well, what do you think I'm doing in here?" I asked, sounding phoney even to my own ears. I tried to make casual conversation. "You're a good spitter," I said to the boy who'd spoken to me, as I eased slowly toward the door. I had to get out of there—fast.

"Hey! Have a good afternoon, guys!" I yelled, bursting out the door. I heard a roar of laughter as I scurried down the hall.

Now where?

I ran into the first room I came to. I flipped the switch and looked around. It was Mrs. D'Agostino's office, the Reading Specialist. I didn't really know her because she helped kids who spoke English as a second language.

I had no idea where she was or when she'd be back. But I had no choice. I had to use this room. I closed the door and took out the stuff. Spidey looked alert.

"Hi, buddy," I whispered. "Don't worry. Everything will be okay."

I sat in Mrs. D'Agostino's chair and picked up the Bug-A-View. I was scared. Scared of it working. Scared of something going wrong.

I had to find a good spot to hide the Bug-A-View so no one would see it (or take it!) if they happened to come into the office. I glanced up at the wall clock. Eight minutes of recess gone. Where would be a good place to transform? I noticed a desk in the back corner. Grabbing the Bug-A-View and the peanut butter jar, I crouched down under the desk. I opened Spidey's jar and laid it down. I pushed the

little red button on the side of the Bug-A-View; the light came on. I held my breath.

Come on, Spidey, come on, I urged him silently. Your favorite spot is all lit up and waiting for you.

The floor was cold and dirty. Spidey was setting a new world's record for slow-moving spiders. I forced myself not to look at the clock.

Finally, he crawled out of his jar and onto the Bug-A-View, inching his way down to the light. I laid my head on the floor and watched Spidey's outline. The light got stronger and brighter and even though I really wanted to keep my eyes open, I had to close them.

I was ready to see the world from a bug's-eye view.

Bombs Away

I blinked my eyes.

All eight of them.

YIPPEE! It worked.

I'd become Spidey.

Okay, it was time to put the search-and-rescue mission into motion and I had to think clearly: I was in Mrs. D'Agostino's office, on the floor, under a desk in the corner. The room looked all fragmented but I started crawling in the direction of a big brown thing that I knew was Mrs. D's desk. I zipped up one of the legs.

On top of the desk, I looked around. My eyes were easier to see through already. I remembered that the window was left of the door when I was sitting on her chair. I wanted to be sure that I didn't get all mixed up about where I was.

The golden blob in the middle of that white mountain

70

looked like it might be the doorknob. I felt for my spinnerets. Ready and waiting.

WHOOSH!

I threw out a monster silk line to the doorknob. It
hooked with a tug. Testing with one of my legs, it felt
strong enough.

GERONIMO!

I was on the knob in seconds. Wow! I scampered down
the door and turned toward the hall. So far so good. Here
goes . . .

THUD!

I just missed being stepped on by a pink leather sneaker
the size of the Titanic. A human wave of girls was line-
dancing down the hall. I felt like my heart was going to
pound out of my chest! This mission was going to be a teeny
bit more difficult than my face-off with Blanche.

I could hear fast music from the gym. Did I dare the
shortcut? It would save some time, but the bodily risks
were pretty high. Oh, what the heck, there were only
twenty-five pairs of feet dancing wildly around the floor.
Plus Suzanne was in there, and I just couldn't resist watching and then telling her about it later.

I zoomed into the gym and climbed high up the wall.
Surveying the room as best as I could, I was relieved to see
no signs of a large beige cowboy hat. But Heidi would be
returning any minute. I watched the scene in front of me
and wished I could laugh. Long ago, people in Sicily believed
that the way to survive a tarantula bite was to dance a

certain folk dance—the tarantella. If you danced hard and fast enough to collapse eventually, you'd be rid of the spider's poison. My classmates had no trouble imagining this: the kids on the floor looked like they'd all gone completely bonkers, flailing their arms and legs around like maniacs, dancing more and more wildly as the music got faster and faster.

I spotted Suzanne's mass of bright orange hair and crossed quickly over to the wall above her. She was dancing with the sissy girls. From my vantage point, I had a perfect aerial view of them. Like all the other kids in the gym, they looked as if they had red biting ants in their pants. Then the music stopped and they all leaned back against the wall, breathing heavily.

I couldn't resist getting a bit closer, and I crawled onto the closet doorknob. Suddenly an enormous pink blob grabbed the knob and shook it. I dug my eight little feet pads in and hung on for dear life. Suzanne was leaning over and laughing, holding the knob to steady herself. Her hand was the pink blob.

When she let go, I jumped off the knob, whizzed across the closet door, and rounded the corner of the gym in no time. Whew! I started down the hallway wall at top speed. Moving like this was an incredible sensation, so fast and smooth it felt like flying. Flinging a silk line across the doorway of Room 28, I missed some kid's head by inches. Yikes! This was a treacherous journey; danger lurked everywhere. I had new admiration for my fellow arthropods—

even with their superpowers, surviving one full day in a school was incredibly difficult.

Finally, I reached the door to my classroom. I zipped inside the room; it was dark and quiet. I waited and listened. Could I sense anything? Not yet. I started down the wall that was behind the display table. Tossing out a silk line across the light switch, I landed smack in the middle of the picture of Abe Lincoln. From this angle, his nose looked pretty scary.

Please, bombardier beetle, talk to me. I thought that as Spidey I'd be able to sense him with something like a mind probe (like I'd just seen on a *Star Trek* rerun). But I couldn't pick up anything.

I was creeping slowly down the wall and then I stopped. The bristly hairs on my legs started to shake slightly. Cautiously, I moved lower.

Now the hairs were prickly and vibrating. My body was on high alert!

Where was he?

And then I saw him, hiding behind the sink faucet. *Yes!* I was weak with relief. He wasn't lost. He wasn't smashed. But he wasn't happy to see me.

Now, not only were my hairy bristles in motion, but my eight legs started trembling.

Because your fearless arthropod leader just remembered something.

This beetle wasn't just any beetle; his insect superpower is one of the most toxic. As in, toxic chemical spray!

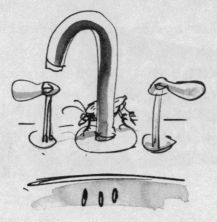

That's right, here I am breezily whizzing around the room, thinking with my boy brain, not realizing what I'm up against in my current body. Because in my current body, I'm facing an insect who can exterminate me.

I gulped.

I didn't know spiders could do that.

And what if the beetle doesn't want to go back into his jar? Would *you* want to go back into *your* jar if you were a beetle? The thought gave me the willies.

And if we didn't agree on the mission here, the beetle would consider me as someone that he might want to guard against.

In other words, he might just drop his own personal atomic bomb on yours truly.

The Deadly Ranger Rick

I couldn't tell if he saw me or not. I crawled slowly down to the other side of the sink so I could face him across it diagonally. I had to stay focused on what I was doing. He has to be brought in alive. That meant I needed to lure him into a trap.

Which could be a little dangerous.

I began to weave my web in strong, tight lines that went in a circular shape, outlining the inside of the sink. Luckily, since I was a cobweb spider, my web was tough and expertly designed, making it almost impossible for a bug to penetrate. The first silk lines, which were held by tiny silk studs, anchored the web. I started on my end of the sink and was making my way rapidly over to where the beetle was. He wasn't facing me but he hadn't moved from his spot. I knew that beetles couldn't see very well; everything was a fuzzy shade of gray to them, which meant that I was a fuzzy gray thing moving toward him.

I finished the outlines and started on the smaller sticky lines that crisscrossed inside the web. Okay, just a little more to go.

Suddenly, the beetle aimed his backside at me.

Pop!

The bomb!

KA-BOOM!

I jumped into the sink, narrowly avoiding the dreaded drain. Above me, the vapor cloud hung in the air. I'd escaped in the nick of time; the pop had alerted me.

I waited, watching the cloud evaporate. Ouch! A few tiny drops of acid dripped on me. Luckily, my skeleton was on the outside of my body, instead of the other way around. The air around me was rippling with heat from the

explosion. And *pee-yew!* They don't call it acid gas for nothing.

Suddenly I realized that now was my chance! It takes a bombardier a little while to recharge after an explosion, so this was it: lure time.

I turned and crawled as quickly as I could toward the beetle. Just close enough to start up those old predator instincts. Because all predators need to find some mouth-watering prey, like a yummy little cobweb spider.

The lure worked! I took off back through the web, knowing *I* wouldn't stick, because all spiders' bodies are covered with a thin layer of oil, to help them in situations like this.

He was right behind me, getting closer, closer. . . .

Fall in the web *now,* fall in the web *now,* fall in the— hooray!

He was stuck; I couldn't sense him behind me anymore. I kept going—just to be safe—then turned around. There he was.

All tied up.

With no place to go.

I did it!

I could see him fighting to get out. My web was amazingly strong—it could hold four thousand times my weight and had the flexibility of a rubber band. I had to fight my instinct to chomp on the beetle first, injecting him with my paralyzing venom. I wanted to try my fangs out so badly!

But I couldn't; he had to be okay.

And I had to get moving.

I zipped up the wall, ready to begin my death-defying journey back to Mrs. D'Agostino's office. Glancing behind, I saw that the beetle was still struggling. I felt bad for him but I knew that he wouldn't have lasted long roaming freely around the school. It was an "it's-for-your-own-good" mission. I guess I'll understand that now when my mom says it to me.

I was perched on a black island in the middle of the white wall when suddenly, a pink blob reached up, causing a shadow to fall over me. I froze, knowing that any sudden movement would make me more obvious. Then I heard a snap and found myself on the floor, which isn't the smartest place to be if you're the size of a Cheerio. The room turned light.

Uh-oh. Mrs. Greene's hand was the pink blob. She'd hit the lights and I was on the switch.

Now she was in the room somewhere.

I scurried over to hide behind a nearby desk leg, waiting until the room was quiet. Okay, the coast seemed clear. Venturing out toward the door, I heard a loud clicking sound. My eight eyes scanned the area.

Enormous, shiny black high heels were moving quickly in my direction.

Mrs. Greene's shoes. I lurched out of her way. I didn't want to collide with them; it wouldn't be much of a match. *Click, click, CLICK!* The heels seemed to be turning in circles, not going in any particular direction. I started crawling quickly away from them, but they seemed to be following me.

STOMP!

One of them crashed down next to me. Then the other. They were huge. They were loud. They were deadly.

HELP! My teacher is trying to squash me!

Where was she going? What was she doing? I tried to fake her out by starting off around one shoe and then quickly darting back through her legs. SMASH! Something just missed me. A magazine. *Ranger Rick.* The one with the leaf-cutter ants on the cover. *I* brought that one from home. SMASH! I scurried up a desk leg.

"Darn spider," I heard her mutter.

Who? Me? SMASH!

The *Ranger Rick* just missed me again.

First an acid bomb and now this.

SMASH! She spotted me again.

I raced up another desk leg. From there, I looked at how far it was across the aisle to the next desk. Could I make it? A silk line would take extra precious seconds. But I couldn't stay on the floor now. I'd have to attempt a jump.

I held my legs together and took a deep breath. GO!

I soared through the air, landing safely on top of the desk. Mrs. Greene was muttering and looking around the floor. I'd thrown her off my trail. I leaped across the rest of the desks until I got to the door. Whew! That was fun! Hey, maybe Spidey's got a little jumping spider in him.

I could hear a loud rumble of voices down one end of the hall. The kids were starting to come back. I looked the opposite way. Clear! I wasn't taking any chances now, zooming on the high walls and avoiding the gym. I was down the hall and rounding the corner in no time.

Mrs. D'Agostino's office seemed like a hundred miles away. I spotted a serious enemy, the school janitor. Just the sight of him wielding that really wide broom and hundred-strand mop made me go even faster. At least I knew exactly where the Bug-A-View was; no one would look under that desk in the corner.

And then a new, horrifying thought made me stop cold: *What if the batteries in the Bug-A-View died?*

I couldn't believe that I hadn't thought of it before. This was, after all, the fourth time I'd used it to transform. And I had to leave it on, with the light shining, because I couldn't exactly push the button when the button was bigger than me.

Did I escape my fate as a fly in order to be Spidey forever? I forced myself toward the open office door on shaky legs. At least Mrs. D wasn't inside.

I'm sorry I ever said the Bug-A-View was a cheap piece of junk. I turned the corner of the door and crawled around

Mrs. D's desk. I was close to the small desk now, I could see the Bug-A-View, but it was turned the other way. I'll never say anything bad about it again. Never.

Taking a deep breath, I zipped under the desk and crawled around the Bug-A-View. The beam of light was as strong as ever. Whew!

Suddenly exhausted, I crawled onto the glass magnifier and closed my eight eyes.

It had been a long half hour.

Was Spiderman Here?

I was back under the desk. Everything worked!

I checked on Spidey; there he was, safe and sound on the end of the Bug-A-View. Picking it up, I gently shook him into his peanut butter jar. Then I packed everything up in my backpack.

As I was crawling out from under the desk, I heard a noise. A squeaky noise. Then another pair of shoes appeared next to mine. They were white, the squeaky nurse-shoe variety. I was concentrating heavily on the details because my brain seemed to be paralyzed. Maybe they were a figment of my imagination.

"Charlie Kaplan? Is that you?" asked Mrs. D'Agostino.

I mumbled something and looked up, widening my eyes in an effort to look innocent.

"What the devil's wrong with your eyes?"

"Um, um. Nothing. Well, er . . ." I stuttered. What to do? Pretend I'm sick? Lost? In need of special reading help? I'm Charlie Kaplan's evil twin?

"Um, um, I got lost."

I didn't look closely but I could tell that she was confused by this answer. "What?"

"I lost my . . . my pencil," I said, straightening up to meet her eye. My mother always told me that people could tell if you're lying because you can't look them in the eye.

"My pencil—it fell out of my backpack and rolled underneath your office door," I said hesitantly. But it didn't sound that bad. "Yeah, that's what happened."

I had now turned around and was walking backward, out of her office, taking baby steps as I spoke. "And while I was picking it up, I decided to take a little walk." I gave her a big smile. Was I making any sense? I had no idea. "I mean, a little walk to the bathroom." My smile was digging into the corners of my face.

"And that's when I got lost. I mean my pencil got lost. I was carrying the pencil to the bathroom, I mean, a pencil was stuck in my shirt pocket." I glanced down. There was no pocket on this shirt!

"I mean my pants pocket and it, I mean, the pencil, fell out of my pants pocket—" I stopped to indicate which pocket—"and rolled under your door."

She was staring at me, her mouth slightly open, as if in a trance. Suddenly I realized that a large beige object had just disappeared around the corner of the hall, in the direction of my classroom.

Heidi!

I looked up at Mrs. D'Agostino and smiled, this time even deeper.

"It's been great talking to you."

Before she could close her mouth, I was history.

But of course, even though I got back a few seconds after Heidi, she'd already heard what happened. Bad news at school travels at record-breaking speed. The rest of my class had just come from recess. Suzanne, who had been standing with the girls, came over to me.

"Heidi knows about the bombardier beetle," she said in a low voice. "Did you find it during recess?"

I opened my mouth to answer, but I didn't know what to say. Heidi walked over to me; she didn't look too happy.

"What happened, Charlie?"

I looked down. "I left the top of the jar open. The bombardier beetle got out." Even though I knew that the beetle would be found soon, the fact remained that I'd screwed up and I had to take responsibility for it. "I'm sorry, Heidi."

The class was quiet. Even Raymond, who usually loved it when someone else got in trouble, was look-

87

ing down at the floor. He knew that dropping the bag of crickets had started this whole mess.

"Well, I'm sure you learned something from this, Charlie," said Heidi. I waited for a lecture but that was all she said. She knew that I felt bad enough; she didn't have to say any more.

I nodded. "Can I look around one more time?"

"Sure," said Heidi, shrugging her shoulders.

Suzanne piped up again. "Where were you? Weren't you supposed to come to the gym?"

"Yeah, it was fun dancing the tarantella," piped up Danny. "You could really let go!"

"Letting go" was Danny's idea of a very good time.

Mrs. Greene was giving us an if-you're-going-to-look-one-more-time-get-moving look, so I started moving in the direction of the sink. It was hard for me to forget that just a few minutes ago, she wanted to smash me. I looked down at her shoes—the heels of doom—and shuddered.

"We've looked over there, Charlie," said Suzanne.

"Maybe he moved," I suggested.

I was now at the sink; Suzanne was next to me. Since I knew the web was there, I could easily make out the white silk lines. Not too shabby, considering I was in a big hurry and it was my first one. Okay, now for the show.

"Suzanne," I said excitedly as I pointed to the sink. "Look!"

Now I could really see my handiwork. The bombardier beetle was still neatly tied up, alive and kicking. I heard Suzanne gasp a little. Heidi, Mrs. Greene, and the rest of the class came over.

"How—? What—?" began Heidi. "I can't believe it!"

"How could this happen?" asked Suzanne. "Wouldn't the beetle spray the spider? Wouldn't the spider bite the beetle?"

Heidi just shook her head in amazement, staring at the web. "I've never seen a spider use his web *just* to tie up an insect, and then not inject venom into it," she said slowly. Then she looked me straight in the eye and smiled slyly. "This is the kind of thing that Spiderman would do, shoot his web out just to trap some bad guys."

"And then leave them hanging there for the cops," added Danny.

Everyone in the class laughed.

The school principal stuck his head into the door-

way of our room. "Professor MacIntosh? Everyone's ready for your lecture in the gym now."

I looked at Mrs. Greene: did she still want me to go to Mr. Baxter's office? This was a perfect opportunity to tell him. Mrs. Greene looked like she was deciding what to do. Finally she gave me a warning look, and I knew I wouldn't have to go. Whew.

Heidi gently touched the web with her fingers, tearing it a bit to pick up the bombardier beetle. "Well, I'm very happy to have this guy back, just in time for my talk," she said. She looked up at me, a smile on her face. "Excellent bug hunting, Bug Boy, excellent bug hunting."

An Old Bug Buddy and a New

"**H**ey, wait up!"

I had just started walking when Suzanne came running up to me. I was surprised; we hadn't walked home together for a while.

"That was really neat what happened in class," she said, catching her breath. "It was amazing that you found the beetle. And the way he was wrapped up! Almost as if the spider knew he shouldn't kill him."

"Yeah," I agreed. You got it exactly right, Suzanne, I thought.

After the beetle was found Heidi gave a great talk and actually got the bombardier to spray out his acid in a kid's hand. She let me display the giant cock-

roach on my shoulder. The students gave her a standing ovation.

Suzanne cleared her throat and then piped up.

"I know I haven't been around much to bug hunt lately," she said. "But I thought you would at least say something."

I didn't know what she was talking about. "About what?"

"That bug thing. What was it called? The Bug-A-View?" she replied.

I stopped and stared at her. I couldn't be hearing this right.

"The Bug-A-View? You sent it?"

She laughed. "Did you think it just appeared on your doorstep? Like magic?"

I was stunned. I looked hard at her. Did she have any idea of its powers?

"When I was visiting my cousins a few weeks ago there was a store near their house called Bug Off, and that's where I found it," she continued. "They had all kinds of bug stuff. When I saw the Bug-A-View, I couldn't resist. It was such a piece of junk. I knew you'd think it was funny." She paused for a moment. "But when you didn't say anything about it I figured that you were mad at me—for hanging around with those girls."

I had stopped walking to listen to her, my brain churning.

"But I told them today that just because *they* don't like bugs doesn't mean *I* can't like them." Suzanne's voice dropped. "And that goes for bug buddies, too."

She gave me a strange look; I realized that she was waiting for me to say something.

"Th-thanks, Suzanne," I stammered, trying to sound normal. "Yeah, I wondered who sent it. It was pretty funny."

We walked on together, both of us quiet. Should I tell her? Suzanne could keep a secret, I knew that for sure. But do I want someone else to know about it?

"Suzanne."

She stopped and looked at me, sensing that this was important. "Yeah?"

I swallowed hard. "The Bug-A-View. It's not just a . . . well, it's got mag—"

"STOP!" A voice yelled. Someone grabbed my arm and jerked me backward. "Don't walk there!"

"Wha—?"

It was Raymond; he was behind us. "Look," he said, pointing down. Suzanne and I leaned over, our heads almost colliding. On the curb was a small spider. My foot was poised over it, ready to make it spider muck. I opened my mouth in amazement. Pain-In? Looking for bugs? Actually stopping me from stepping on one instead of stepping on it first?

Suzanne picked up the spider in her hand and looked around. "Hey, we're at my street already."

She passed the spider to me. I took a close look at him.

"Bye, guys," Suzanne called, starting down her block. "See you tomorrow." Then she stopped and turned around. "Thanks, Raymond. Great bug watching."

Raymond almost glowed he looked so happy. We watched Suzanne walk to her house. I would have to tell her about the Bug-A-View tomorrow. Maybe.

"You and Suzanne stopped and I didn't want you to think I was following you or something, so I retied my shoe. When I bent down, there he was, and there *you* were—or rather there your foot was."

We both laughed. I guess he could be okay. It sure had been a day of surprises.

We walked the rest of the way home together. As we got near to Raymond's house, he stopped.

"Do you want to see something neat?"

"Sure," I answered.

We walked around to a big maple tree that was in his backyard. Raymond pointed proudly to the base of the tree. On the ground, in and around the mass of roots, there was a gigantic anthill. Hundreds of ants were scurrying all over the place, carrying leaves, parts of bugs—all sorts of stuff.

"Wow," I said, crouching down for a better look. "This is one of the biggest ant colonies I've ever seen. Look," I said, pointing at a large ant with a big head and jaw. "That's a soldier ant. He's—"

"I know," Raymond interrupted. "Protecting the queen. When I first discovered it, I did some reading. Ants are amazing."

"They are," I agreed. "Maybe one day you could come over and help me feed my ant-lion larvae."

"That would be great," said Raymond, with a big smile on his face.

I turned to go. My mother would be getting worried. We walked out of the yard.

"Hey, Charlie," Raymond called as I started up my front walk. "Can you imagine what it's like to be an ant, living in one of those huge colonies with hundreds of other ants?"

I looked at him, nodded, and smiled.

I sure could.

About the Author

Carol Sonenklar

The insect fair in *Bug Boy* is based on the insect fair that's held every year at Pennsylvania State University. In addition to bug lectures, artwork, and collections, there are unusual events like cockroach races, a "buggy" petting zoo, and the ever-popular insect cuisine.

My son, Sam, always eager to try anything bug-related, downed several chocolate-covered crickets, took a couple of sips of wax-moth-caterpillar chowder, and then moved on to the stir-fried mealworms. The entomologist behind the counter explained that it was made with onions, garlic, mushrooms, and meal-worms. He handed Sam a cracker. Sam looked at it, made a face, and handed it to me.

"I can't eat this."

"Why? What's wrong?"

"Mom, you know I hate mushrooms."

So I removed the mushrooms and he happily munched away.

Betsy Lewin

Once I was a judge in a local pet show that included every kind of animal imaginable—from the usual array of cats and dogs to more exotic pets like snakes and parrots.

There were prizes for the biggest short-haired pet and the smallest long-haired pet, for the longest ears, and for the shortest tail, to name a few. In the category "pet with the most pleasing expression," I voted for the tarantula. And it won.